The Little Men

BIBLIOMYSTERY SERIES

#1 Ken Bruen, *The Book of Virtue,* $4.95
#2 Reed Farrel Coleman, *The Book of Ghosts,* $4.95
#3 Anne Perry, *The Scroll,* $4.95
#4 Nelson DeMille, *The Book Case,* $6.95
#5 C.J. Box, *Pronghorns of the Third Reich,* $4.95
#6 William Link, *Death Leaves a Bookmark,* $4.95
#7 Jeffery Deaver, *An Acceptable Sacrifice,* $5.95
#8 Loren D. Estleman, *Book Club,* $4.95
#9 Laura Lippman, *The Book Thing,* $4.95
#10 Andrew Taylor, *The Long Sonata of the Dead*, $4.95
#11 Peter Blauner, *The Final Testament*, $4.95
#12 John Connolly, *The Caxton Lending Library & Book Depository*, $6.95
#13 David Bell, *Rides a Stranger*, $4.95
#14 Thomas H. Cook, *What's in a Name?*, $4.95
#15 Mickey Spillane & Max Allan Collins, *It's in the Book*, $4.95
#16 Peter Lovesey, *Remaindered*, $5.95
#17 F. Paul Wilson *The Compendium of Srem*, $5.95
#18 Lyndsay Faye, *The Gospel of Sheba*, $5.95
#19 Bradford Morrow, *The Nature of My Inheritance*, $5.95
#20 R.L. Stine, *The Sequel*, $4.95
#21 Joyce Carol Oates, *Mystery, Inc.,* $6.95
#22 Thomas Perry, *The Book of the Lion,* $5.95
#23 Elizabeth George, *The Mysterious Disappearance of the Reluctant Book Fairy*, $6.95
#24 Carolyn Hart, *From the Queen,* $5.95
#25 Megan Abbott, *The Little Men,* $5.95

The Little Men

By
Megan Abbott

Mysterious Bookshop

New York

The Little Men
by Megan Abbott

Copyright © 2015

All rights reserved. Permission to reprint,
in whole or in part,
should be addressed to:
Otto Penzler
The Mysterious Bookshop
58 Warren Street
New York, N.Y. 10007
Ottopenzler@mysteriousbookshop.com

ISBN (978-1-61316-076-3) (limited edition)
ISBN (978-1-61316-075-6) (paperback)

The
Little Men

*A*t night, the sounds from the canyon shifted and changed. The bungalow seemed to lift itself with every echo and the walls were breathing. Panting.

Just after two, she'd wake, her eyes stinging, as if someone had waved a flashlight across them.

And then, she'd hear the noise.

Every night.

The tapping noise, like a small animal trapped behind the wall.

That was what it reminded her of. Like when she was a girl, and that possum got caught in the crawlspace. For weeks, they just heard scratching. They only found it when the walls started to smell.

It's not the little men, she told herself. *It's not.*

And then she'd hear a whimper and startle

herself. Because it was her whimper and she was so frightened.

I'm not afraid I'm not I'm not

It had begun four months ago, the day Penny first set foot in the Canyon Arms. The chocolate and pink bungalows, the high arched windows and French doors, the tiled courtyard, cosseted on all sides by eucalyptus, pepper, and olive trees, miniature date palms—it was like a dream of a place, not a place itself.

This is what it was supposed to be, she thought.

The Hollywood she'd always imagined, the Hollywood of her childhood imagination, assembled from newsreels: Kay Francis in silver lamé and Clark Gable driving down Sunset in his Duesenberg, everyone beautiful and everything possible.

That world, if it ever really existed, was long gone by the time she'd arrived on that Greyhound a half-dozen years ago. It had been swallowed up by the clatter and color of 1953 Hollywood, with its swooping motel roofs and shiny glare of its hamburger stands and drive-ins, and its descending smog, which made her throat burn at night. Sometimes she could barely breathe.

But here in this tucked away courtyard,

deep in Beachwood Canyon, it was as if that Old Hollywood still lingered, even bloomed. The smell of apricot hovered, the hush and echoes of the canyons soothed. You couldn't hear a horn honk, a brake squeal. Only the distant *ting-ting* of window chimes, somewhere. One might imagine a peignoired Norma Shearer drifting through the rounded doorway of one of the bungalows, cocktail shaker in hand.

"It's perfect," Penny whispered, her heels tapping on the Mexican tiles. "I'll take it."

"That's fine," said the landlady, Mrs. Stahl, placing Penny's cashier's check in the drooping pocket of her satin housecoat and handing her the keyring, heavy in her palm.

The scent, thick with pollen and dew, was enough to make you dizzy with longing.

And so close to the Hollywood sign, visible from every vantage, which had to mean something.

She had found it almost by accident, tripping out of the Carnival Tavern after three stingers.

"We've all been stood up," the waitress had tut-tutted, snapping the bill holder at her hip. "But we still pay up."

"I wasn't stood up," Penny said. After all, Mr. D. had called, the hostess summoning

Penny to one of the hot telephone booths. Penny was still tugging her skirt free from its door hinges when he broke it to her.

He wasn't coming tonight and wouldn't be coming again. He had many reasons why, beginning with his busy work schedule, the demands of the studio, plus negotiations with the union were going badly. By the time he got around to the matter of his wife and six children, she wasn't listening, letting the phone drift from her ear.

Gazing through the booth's glass accordion doors, she looked out at the long row of spinning lanterns strung along the bar's windows. They reminded her of the magic lamp she had when she was small, scattering galloping horses across her bedroom walls.

You could see the Carnival Tavern from miles away because of the lanterns. It was funny seeing them up close, the faded circus clowns silhouetted on each. They looked so much less glamorous, sort of shabby. She wondered how long they'd been here, and if anyone even noticed them anymore.

She was thinking all these things while Mr. D. was still talking, his voice hoarse with logic and finality. A faint aggression.

He concluded by saying surely she agreed that all the craziness had to end.

You were a luscious piece of candy, he said, *but now I gotta spit you out.*

After, she walked down the steep exit ramp from the bar, the lanterns shivering in the canyon breeze.

And she walked and walked and that was how she found the Canyon Arms, tucked off behind hedges so deep you could disappear into them. The smell of the jasmine so strong she wanted to cry.

"You're an actress, of course," Mrs. Stahl said, walking her to Bungalow Number Four.

"Yes," she said. "I mean, no." Shaking her head. She felt like she was drunk. It was the apricot. No, Mrs. Stahl's cigarette. No, it was her lipstick. Tangee, with its sweet orange smell, just like Penny's own mother.

"Well," Mrs. Stahl said. "We're all actresses, I suppose."

"I used to be," Penny finally managed. "But I got practical. I do makeup now. Over at Republic."

Mrs. Stahl's eyebrows, thin as seaweed, lifted. "Maybe you could do me sometime."

It was the beginning of something, she was sure.

No more living with sundry starlets stacked bunk-to-bunk in one of those stucco boxes in

West Hollywood. The Sham-Rock. The Sun-Kist Villa. The smell of cold cream and last night's sweat, a brush of talcum powder between the legs.

She hadn't been sure she could afford to live alone, but Mrs. Stahl's rent was low. Surprisingly low. And, if the job at Republic didn't last, she still had her kitty, which was fat these days on account of those six months with Mr. D., a studio man with a sofa in his office that wheezed and puffed. Even if he really meant what he said, that it really was kaput, she still had that last check he'd given her. He must have been planning the brush off, because it was the biggest yet, and made out to cash.

And the Canyon Arms had other advantages. Number Four, like all the bungalows, was already furnished: sun-bleached zebra print sofa and key lime walls, that bright-white kitchen with its cherry-sprigged wallpaper. The first place she'd ever lived that didn't have rust stains in the tub or the smell of moth balls everywhere.

And there were the built-in bookshelves filled with novels in crinkling dustjackets.

She liked books, especially the big ones by Lloyd C. Douglas or Frances Parkinson Keyes, though the books in Number Four were all at least twenty years old with a sleek, high-tone look about them. The kind without any people on the cover.

She vowed to read them all during her time at the Canyon Arms. Even the few tucked in the back, the ones with brown-paper covers.

In fact, she started with those. Reading them late at night, with a pink gin conjured from grapefruit peel and an old bottle of Gilbey's she found in the cupboard. Those books gave her funny dreams.

"She got one."

Penny turned on her heels, one nearly catching on one of the courtyard tiles. But, looking around, she didn't see anyone. Only an open window, smoke rings emanating like a dragon's mouth.

"She finally got one," the voice came again.

"Who's there?" Penny said, squinting toward the window.

An old man leaned forward from his perch just inside Number Three, the bungalow next door. He wore a velvet smoking jacket faded to a deep rose.

"And a pretty one at that," he said, smiling with graying teeth. "How do you like Number Four?"

"I like it very much," she said. She could

hear something rustling behind him in his bungalow. "It's perfect for me."

"I believe it is," he said, nodding slowly. "Of that I am sure."

The rustle came again. Was it a roommate? A pet? It was too dark to tell. When it came once more, it was almost like a voice shushing.

"I'm late," she said, taking a step back, her heel caving slightly.

"Oh," he said, taking a puff. "Next time."

That night, she woke, her mouth dry from gin, at two o'clock. She had been dreaming she was on an exam table and a doctor with an enormous head mirror was leaning so close to her she could smell his gum: violet. The ringlight at its center seemed to spin, as if to hypnotize her.

She saw spots even when she closed her eyes again.

The next morning, the man in Number Three was there again, shadowed just inside the window frame, watching the comings and goings on the courtyard.

Head thick from last night's gin and two morning cigarettes, Penny was feeling what her mother used to call "the hickedty ticks."

So, when she saw the man, she stopped and said briskly, "What did you mean yesterday? 'She finally got one'?"

He smiled, laughing without any noise, his shoulders shaking.

"Mrs. Stahl got one, got you," he said. "As in: Will you walk into my parlor? said the spider to the fly."

When he leaned forward, she could see the stripes of his pajama top through the shiny threads of his velvet sleeve. His skin was rosy and wet looking.

"I'm no chump, if that's your idea. It's good rent. I know good rent."

"I bet you do, my girl. I bet you do. Why don't you come inside for a cup? I'll tell you a thing or two about this place. And about your Number Four."

The bungalow behind him was dark, with something shining beside him. A bottle, or something else.

"We all need something," he added cryptically, winking.

She looked at him. "Look, mister—"

"Flant. Mr. Flant. Come inside, miss. Open the front door. I'm harmless." He waved his pale pink hand, gesturing toward his lap mysteriously.

Behind him, she thought she saw something moving in the darkness over his slouching shoulders. And music playing softly. And old song about setting the world on fire, or not.

Mr. Flant was humming with it, his body soft with age and stillness, but his milky eyes insistent and penetrating.

A breeze lifted and the front door creaked open several inches, and the scent of tobacco and bay rum nearly overwhelmed her.

"I don't know," she said, even as she moved forward.

Later, she would wonder why, but in that moment, she felt it was definitely the right thing to do.

The other man in Number Three was not as old as Mr. Flant but still much older than Penny. Wearing only an undershirt and trousers, he had a moustache and big round shoulders that looked gray with old sweat. When he smiled, which was often, she could tell he was once matinee-idol handsome, with the outsized head of all movie stars.

"Call me Benny," he said, handing her a coffee cup that smelled strongly of rum.

Mr. Flant was explaining that Number Four had been empty for years because of something that happened there a long time ago.

"Sometimes she gets a tenant," Benny reminded Mr. Flant. "The young musician with the sweaters."

"That did not last long," Mr. Flant said.

"What happened?"

"The police came. He tore out a piece of the wall with his bare hands."

Penny's eyebrows lifted.

Benny nodded. "His fingers were hanging like clothespins."

"But I don't understand. What happened in Number Four?"

"Some people let the story get to them," Benny said, shaking his head.

"What story?"

The two men looked at each other.

Mr. Flant rotated his cup in his hand.

"There was a death," he said softly. "A man who lived there, a dear man. Lawrence was his name. Larry. A talented bookseller. He died."

"Oh."

"Boy did he," Benny said. "Gassed himself."

"At the Canyon Arms?" she asked, feeling sweat on her neck despite all the fans blowing everywhere, lifting motes and old skin. That's what dust really is, you know, one of her roommates once told her, blowing it from her fingertips. "Inside my bungalow?"

They both nodded gravely.

"They carried him out through the courtyard," Mr. Flant said, staring vaguely out the window. "That great sheaf of blond hair of his. Oh, my."

"So it's a challenge for some people," Benny said. "Once they know."

Penny remembered the neighbor boy who fell from their tree and died from blood poisoning two days later. No one would eat its pears after that.

"Well," she said, eyes drifting to the smudgy window, "some people are superstitious."

Soon, Penny began stopping by Number Three a few mornings a week, before work. Then, the occasional evening, too. They served rye or applejack.

It helped with her sleep. She didn't remember her dreams, but her eyes still stung lightspots most nights.

Sometimes the spots took odd shapes and she would press her fingers against her lids trying to make them stop.

"You could come to my bungalow," she offered once. But they both shook their heads slowly, and in unison.

Mostly, they spoke of Lawrence. Larry. Who seemed like such a sensitive soul, delicately formed and too fine for this town.

"When did it happen?" Penny asked, feeling dizzy, wishing Benny had put more water in the applejack. "When did he die?"

"Just before the war. A dozen years ago."

"He was only thirty-five."

"That's so sad," Penny said, finding her eyes misting, the liquor starting to tell on her.

"His bookstore is still on Cahuenga Boulevard," Benny told her. "He was so proud when it opened."

"Before that, he sold books for Stanley Rose," Mr. Flant added, sliding a handkerchief from under the cuff of his fraying sleeve. "Larry was very popular. Very attractive. An accent soft as a Carolina pine."

"He'd pronounce 'bed' like 'bay-ed.'" Benny grinned, leaning against the window sill and smiling that Gable smile. "And he said 'bay-ed' a lot."

"I met him even before he got the job with Stanley," Mr. Flant said, voice speeding up. "Long before Benny."

Benny shrugged, topping off everyone's drinks.

"He was selling books out of the trunk of his old Ford," Mr. Flant continued. "That's where I first bought *Ulysses*."

Benny grinned again. "He sold me my first Tijuana Bible. *Dagwood Has a Family Party*."

13

Mr. Flant nodded, laughed. "*Popeye in The Art of Love*. It staggered me. He had an uncanny sense. He knew just what you wanted."

They explained that Mr. Rose, whose bookstore once graced Hollywood Boulevard and had attracted great talents, used to send young Larry to the studios with a suitcase full of books. His job was to trap and mount the big shots. Show them the goods, sell them books by the yard, art books they could show off in their offices, dirty books they could hide in their big gold safes.

Penny nodded. She was thinking about the special books Mr. D. kept in his office, behind the false encyclopedia fronts. The books had pictures of girls doing things with long, fuzzy fans and peacock feathers, a leather crop.

She wondered if Larry had sold them to him.

"To get to those guys, he had to climb the satin rope," Benny said. "The studio secretaries, the script girls, the publicity office, even makeup girls like you. Hell, the grips. He loved a sexy grip."

"This town can make a whore out of anyone," Penny found herself blurting.

She covered her mouth, ashamed, but both men just laughed.

Mr. Flant looked out the window into the courtyard, the *flip-flipping* of banana leaves against the shutter. "I think he loved the actresses the most, famous or not."

"He said he liked the feel of a woman's skin in 'bay-ed,'" Benny said, rubbing his left arm, his eyes turning dark, soft. "'Course, he'd slept with his mammy until he was thirteen."

As she walked back to her own bungalow, she always had the strange feeling she might see Larry. That he might emerge behind the rose bushes or around the statue of Venus.

Once she looked down into the fountain basin and thought she could see his face instead of her own.

But she didn't even know what he looked like.

Back in the bungalow, head fuzzy and the canyon so quiet, she thought about him more. The furniture, its fashion at least two decades past, seemed surely the same furniture he'd known. Her hands on the smooth bands of the rattan sofa. Her feet, her toes on the banana silk tassels of the rug. And the old mirror in the bathroom, its tiny black pocks.

In the late hours, lying on the bed, the mattress too soft, with a vague smell of mildew, she found herself waking again and again, each time with a start.

It always began with her eyes stinging, dreaming again of a doctor with the head mirror, or a car careering toward her on the highway, always lights in her face.

One night, she caught the lights moving, her eyes landing on the far wall, the baseboards.

For several moments, she'd see the light spots, fuzzed and floating, as if strung together by the thinnest of threads.

The spots began to look like the darting mice that sometimes snuck inside her childhood home. She never knew mice could be that fast. So fast that if she blinked, she'd miss them, until more came. Was that what it was?

If she squinted hard, they even looked like little men. Could it be mice on their hindfeet?

The next morning, she set traps.

"I'm sorry, he's unavailable," the receptionist said. Even over the phone, Penny knew which one. The beauty marks and giraffe neck.

"But listen," Penny said, "it's not like he thinks. I'm just calling about the check he gave me. The bank stopped payment on it."

So much for Mr. D.'s parting gift for their

time together. She was going to use it to make rent, to buy a new girdle, maybe even a television set.

"I've passed along your messages, Miss Smith. That's really all I can do."

"Well, that's not all I can do," Penny said, her voice trembling. "You tell him that."

Keeping busy was the only balm. At work, it was easy, the crush of people, the noise and personality of the crew.

Nights were when the bad thoughts came, and she knew she shouldn't let them.

In the past, she'd had those greasy-skinned roommates to drown out thinking. They all had rashes from cheap studio makeup and the clap from cheap studio men and beautiful figures like Penny's own. And they never stopped talking, twirling their hair in curlers and licking their fingers to turn the magazine pages. But their chatter-chatter-chatter muffled all Penny's thoughts. And the whole atmosphere—the thick muzz of Woolworth's face powder and nylon nighties when they even shared a bed—made everything seem cheap and lively and dumb and easy and light.

Here, in the bungalow, after leaving Mr. Flant and Benny to drift off into their applejack dreams, Penny had only herself. And the books.

Late into the night, waiting for the lightspots to come, she found her eyes wouldn't shut. They started twitching all the time, and maybe it was the night jasmine, or the beachburr.

But she had the books. All those books, these beautiful, brittling books, books that made her feel things, made her long to go places and see things—the River Liffey and Paris, France.

And then there were those in the wrappers, the brown paper soft at the creases, the white baker string slightly fraying.

Her favorite was about a detective recovering stolen jewels from an unlikely hiding spot.

But there was one that frightened her. About a farmer's daughter who fell asleep each night on a bed of hay. And in the night, the hay came alive, poking and stabbing at her.

It was supposed to be funny, but it gave Penny bad dreams.

"Well, she was in love with Larry," Mr. Flant said. "But she was not Larry's kind."

Penny had been telling them how Mrs. Stahl had shown up at her door the night before, in worn satin pajamas and cold cream, to scold her for moving furniture around.

"I don't even know how she saw," Penny said. "I just pushed the bed away from the wall."

She had lied, telling Mrs. Stahl she could hear the oven damper popping at night. She was afraid to tell her about the shadows and lights and other things that made no sense in daytime. Like the mice moving behind the wall on hindfeet, so agile she'd come to think of them as pixies, dwarves. Little men.

"It's not your place to move things," Mrs. Stahl had said, quite loudly, and for a moment Penny thought the woman might cry.

"That's all his furniture, you know," Benny said. "Larry's. Down to the forks and spoons."

Penny felt her teeth rattle slightly in her mouth.

"He gave her books she liked," Benny added. "Stiff British stuff he teased her about. Charmed himself out of the rent for months."

"When he died she wailed around the courtyard for weeks," Mr. Flant recalled. "She wanted to scatter the ashes into the canyon."

"But his people came instead," Benny said. "Came on a train all the way from Carolina. A man and woman with cardboard suitcases packed with pimento sandwiches. They took the body home."

"They said Hollywood had killed him."

Benny shook his head, smiled that tobacco-toothed smile of his. "They always say that."

"You're awfully pretty for a face-fixer," one of the actors told her, fingers wagging beneath his long makeup bib.

Penny only smiled, and scooted before the pinch came.

It was a Western, so it was mostly men, whiskers, lip bristle, three-day beards filled with dust.

Painting the girl's faces was harder. They all had ideas of how they wanted it. They were hard girls, striving to get to Paramount, to MGM. Or started out there and hit the Republic rung on the long slide down. To Allied, AIP. Then studios no one ever heard of, operating out of some slick guy's house in the Valley.

They had bad teeth and head lice and some had smells on them when they came to the studio, like they hadn't washed properly. The costume assistants always pinched their noses behind their backs.

It was a rough town for pretty girls. The only place it was.

Penny knew she had lost her shine long ago. Many men had rubbed it off, shimmy by shimmy.

But it was just as well, and she'd just as soon be in the warpaint business. When it rubbed off the girls, she could just get out her brushes, her power puffs, and shine them up like new.

As she tapped the powder pots, though, her mind would wander. She began thinking about Larry bounding through the backlots. Would he have come to Republic with his wares? Maybe. Would he have soft-soaped her, hoping her bosses might have a taste for T.S. Eliot or a French deck?

By day, she imagined him as a charmer, a cheery, silver-tongued roué.

But at night, back at the Canyon Arms, it was different.

You see, sometimes she thought she could see him moving, room to room, his face pale, his trousers soiled. Drinking and crying over someone, something, whatever he'd lost that he was sure wasn't ever coming back.

There were sounds now. Sounds to go with the two a.m. lights, or the mice or whatever they were.

Tap-tap-tap.

At first, she thought she was only hearing

the banana trees, brushing against the side of the bungalow. Peering out the window, the moon-filled courtyard, she couldn't tell. The air looked very still.

Maybe, she thought, it's the fan palms outside the kitchen window, so much lush foliage everywhere, just the thing she'd loved, but now it seemed to be touching her constantly, closing in.

And she didn't like to go into the kitchen at night. The white tile glowed eerily, reminded her of something. The wide expanse of Mr. D.'s belly, his shirt pushed up, his watch chain hanging. The coaster of milk she left for the cat the morning she ran away from home. For Hollywood.

The mouse traps never caught anything. Every morning, after the rumpled sleep and all the flits and flickers along the wall, she moved them to different places. She looked for signs.

She never saw any.

One night, three a.m., she knelt down on the floor, running her fingers along the baseboards. With her ear to the wall, she thought the tapping might be coming from inside. A *tap-tap-tap*. Or was it a *tick-tick-tick*?

"I've never heard anything here," Mr. Flant

told her the following day, "but I take sedatives."

Benny wrinkled his brow. "Once, I saw pink elephants," he offered. "You think that might be it?"

Penny shook her head. "It's making it hard to sleep."

"Dear," Mr. Flant said, "would you like a little helper?"

He held out his palm, pale and moist. In the center, a white pill shone.

That night she slept impossibly deeply. So deeply she could barely move, her neck twisted and locked, her body hunched inside itself.

Upon waking, she threw up in the waste basket.

That evening, after work, she waited in the courtyard for Mrs. Stahl.

Smoking cigarette after cigarette, Penny noticed things she hadn't before. Some of the tiles in the courtyard were cracked, some missing. She hadn't noticed that before. Or the chips and gouges on the sculpted lions on the center fountain, their mouths spouting only a trickle of acid green. The drain at the bottom of the fountain, clogged with crushed cigarette packs, a used contraceptive.

Finally, she saw Mrs. Stahl saunter into view, a large picture hat wilting across her tiny head.

"Mrs. Stahl," she said, "have you ever had an exterminator come?"

The woman stopped, her entire body still for a moment, her left hand finally rising to her face, brushing her hair back under her mustard-colored scarf.

"I run a clean residence," she said, voice low in the empty, sunlit courtyard. That courtyard, oleander and wisteria everywhere, bright and poisonous, like everything in this town.

"I can hear something behind the wainscoting," Penny replied. "Maybe mice, or maybe it's baby possums caught in the wall between the bedroom and kitchen."

Mrs. Stahl looked at her. "Is it after you bake? It might be the dampers popping again."

"I'm not much of a cook. I haven't even turned on the oven yet."

"That's not true," Mrs. Stahl said, lifting her chin triumphantly. "You had it on the other night."

"What?" Then Penny remembered. It had rained sheets and she'd used it to dry her dress. But it had been very late and she didn't see how Mrs. Stahl could know. "Are you peeking in my windows?" she asked, voice tightening.

"I saw the light. The oven door was open. You shouldn't do that," Mrs. Stahl said, shaking her head. "It's very dangerous."

"You're not the first landlord I caught peeping. I guess I need to close my curtains," Penny said coolly. "But it's not the oven damper I'm hearing each and every night. I'm telling you: there's something inside my walls. Something in the kitchen."

Mrs. Stahl's mouth seemed to quiver slightly, which emboldened Penny.

"Do I need to get out the ball peen I found under the sink and tear a hole in the kitchen wall, Mrs. Stahl?"

"Don't you dare!" she said, clutching Penny's wrist, her costume rings digging in. "Don't you dare!"

Penny felt the panic on her, the woman's breaths coming in sputters. She insisted they both sit on the fountain edge.

For a moment, they both just breathed, the apricot-perfumed air thick in Penny's lungs.

"Mrs. Stahl, I'm sorry. It's just—I need to sleep."

Mrs. Stahl took a long breath, then her eyes narrowed again. "It's those chinwags next door, isn't it? They've been filling your ear with bile."

"What? Not about this, I—"

"I had the kitchen cleaned thoroughly after it happened. I had it cleaned, the linoleum stripped out. I put up fresh wallpaper over every square inch after it happened. I covered everything with wallpaper."

"Is that where it happened?" Penny asked. "That poor man who died in Number Four? Larry?"

But Mrs. Stahl couldn't speak, or wouldn't, breathing into her handkerchief, lilac silk, the small square over her mouth suctioning open and closed, open and closed.

"He was very beautiful," she finally whispered. "When they pulled him out of the oven, his face was the most exquisite red. Like a ripe, ripe cherry."

Knowing how it happened changed things. Penny had always imagined handsome, melancholy Larry walking around the apartment, turning gas jets on. Settling into that club chair in the living room. Or maybe settling in bed and slowly drifting from earth's fine tethers.

She wondered how she could ever use the oven now, or even look at it.

It had to be the same one. That Magic Chef, which looked like the one from childhood, white porcelain and cast iron. Not like those new slabs, buttercup or mint green.

The last tenant, Mr. Flant told her later, smelled gas all the time.

"She said it gave her headaches," he said. "Then one night she came here, her face white as snow. She said she'd just seen St. Agatha in the kitchen, with her bloody breasts."

"I . . . I don't see anything like that," Penny said.

Back in the bungalow, trying to sleep, she began picturing herself the week before. How she'd left that oven door open, her fine, rain-slicked dress draped over the rack. The truth was, she'd forgotten about it, only returning for it hours later.

Walking to the closet now, she slid the dress from its hanger pressing it to her face. But she couldn't smell anything.

Mr. D. still had not returned her calls. The bank had charged her for the bounced check so she'd have to return the hat she'd bought, and rent was due again in two days.

When all the other crew members were making their way to the commissary for lunch, Penny slipped away and splurged on cab fare to the studio.

As she opened the door to his outer office, the receptionist was already on her feet and walking purposefully toward Penny.

"Miss," she said, nearly blocking Penny, "you're going to have to leave. Mac shouldn't have let you in downstairs."

"Why not? I've been here dozens of—"

"You're not on the appointment list, and that's our system now, Miss."

"Does he have an appointment list now for that squeaking starlet sofa in there?" Penny asked, jerking her arm and pointing at the leather-padded door. A man with a thin moustache and a woman in a feathered hat looked up from their magazines.

The receptionist was already on the phone. "Mac, I need you . . . Yes, that one."

"If he thinks he can just toss me out like street trade," she said, marching over and thumping on Mr. D.'s door, "he'll be very, very sorry."

Her knuckles made no noise in the soft leather. Nor did her fist.

"Miss," someone said. It was the security guard striding toward her.

"I'm allowed to be here," she insisted, her voice tight and high. "I did my time. I earned the right."

But the guard had his hand on her arm.

Desperate, she looked down at the man and the woman waiting. Maybe she thought they would help. But why would they?

The woman pretended to be absorbed in her *Cinestar* magazine.

But the man smiled at her, hair oil gleaming. And winked.

The next morning she woke bleary but determined. She would forget about Mr. D. She didn't need his money. After all, she had a job, a good one.

It was hot on the lot that afternoon, and none of the makeup crew could keep the dust off the faces. There were so many lines and creases on every face—you never think about it until you're trying to make everything smooth.

"Penny," Gordon, the makeup supervisor said. She had the feeling he'd been watching her for several moments as she pressed the powder into the actor's face, holding it still.

"It's so dusty," she said, "so it's taking a while."

He waited until she finished then, as the actor walked away, he leaned forward.

"Everything all right, Pen?"

He was looking at something—her neck, her chest.

"What do you mean?" she said, setting the powder down.

But he just kept looking at her.

"Working on your carburetor, beautiful?" one of the grips said, as he walked by.

"What? I . . ."

Peggy turned to the makeup mirror. That was when she saw the long grease smear on her collarbone. And the line of black soot across her hairline too.

"I don't know," Penny said, her voice sounding slow and sleepy. "I don't have a car."

Then, it came to her: the dream she'd had in the early morning hours. That she was in the kitchen, checking on the oven damper. The squeak of the door on its hinges, and Mrs. Stahl outside the window, her eyes glowing like a wolf's.

"It was a dream," she said, now. Or was it? Had she been sleepwalking the night before?

Had she been in the kitchen . . . *at the oven* . . . in her sleep?

"Penny," Gordon said, looking at her squintily. "Penny, maybe you should go home."

It was so early, and Penny didn't want to go back to Canyon Arms. She didn't want to go inside Number Four, or walk past the kitchen, its cherry wallpaper lately giving her the feeling of blood spatters.

Also, lately, she kept thinking she saw Mrs. Stahl peering at her between the wooden blinds as she watered the banana trees.

Instead, she took the bus downtown to the big library on South Fifth. She had an idea.

The librarian, a boy with a bowtie, helped her find the obituaries.

She found three about Larry, but none had photos, which was disappointing.

The one in the *Mirror* was the only with any detail, any texture.

It mentioned that the body had been found by the "handsome proprietress, one Mrs. Herman Stahl," who "fell to wailing" so loud it was heard all through the canyons, up the promontories and likely high into the mossed eaves of the Hollywood sign.

"So what happened to Mrs. Stahl's husband?" Penny asked when she saw Mr. Flant and Benny that night.

"He died just a few months before Larry," Benny said. "Bad heart, they say."

Mr. Flant raised one pale eyebrow. "She never spoke of him. Only of Larry."

"He told me once she watched him, Larry

did," Benny said. "She watched him through his bedroom blinds. While he made love."

Instantly, Penny knew this was true.

She thought of herself in that same bed each night, the mattress so soft, its posts sometimes seeming to curl inward.

Mrs. Stahl had insisted Penny move it back against the wall. Penny refused, but the next day she came home to find the woman moving it herself, her short arms spanning the mattress, her face pressed into its applique.

Watching, Penny had felt like the Peeping Tom. It was so intimate.

"Sometimes I wonder," Mr. Flant said now. "There were rumors. Black Widow, or Old Maid."

"You can't make someone put his head in the oven," Benny said. "At least not for long. The gas'd get at you, too."

"True," Mr. Flant said.

"Maybe it didn't happen at the oven," Penny blurted. "She found the body. What if she just turned on the gas while he was sleeping?"

"And dragged him in there, for the cops?"

Mr. Flant and Benny looked at each other.

"She's very strong," Penny said.

Back in her bungalow, Penny sat just inside her bedroom window, waiting.

Peering through the blinds, long after midnight, she finally saw her. Mrs. Stahl, walking along the edges of the courtyard.

She was singing softly and her steps were uneven and Penny thought she might be tight, but it was hard to know.

Penny was developing a theory.

Picking up a book, she made herself stay awake until two.

Then, slipping from bed, she tried to follow the flashes of light, the shadows.

Bending down, she put her hand on the baseboards, as if she could touch those funny shapes, like mice on their haunches. Or tiny men, marching.

"Something's there!" she said outloud, her voice surprising her. "It's in the walls."

In the morning, it would all be blurry, but in that moment, clues were coming together in her head, something to do with gas jets and Mrs. Stahl and love gone awry and poison in the walls, and she had figured it out before anything bad had happened.

It made so much sense in the moment, and when the sounds came too, the little *tap-taps* behind the plaster, she nearly cheered.

Mr. Flant poured her glass after glass of amaro. Benny waxed his moustache and showed Penny his soft shoe.

They were trying to make her feel better about losing her job.

"I never came in late except two or three times. I always did my job," Penny said, biting her lip so hard it bled. "I think I know who's responsible. He kited me for seven hundred and forty dollars and now he's out to ruin me."

Then she told them how, a few days ago, she had written him a letter.

Mr. D.—

I don't write to cause you any trouble. What's mine is mine and I never knew you for an indian giver.

I bought fine dresses to go to Hollywood Park with you, to be on your arm at Villa Capri. I had to buy three stockings a week, your clumsy hands pawing at them. I had to turn down jobs and do two cycles of penicillin because of you. Also because of you, I got the heave-ho from my roommate Pauline who said you fondled her by the dumbwaiter. So that money is the least a gentleman could offer a lady. The least, Mr.D.

Let me ask you: those books you kept behind the false bottom in your desk drawer on the lot—did you buy those from Mr. Stanley Rose, or his handsome assistant Larry?

I wonder if your wife knows the kinds of books you keep in your office, the girls you keep there and make do shameful things?

I know Larry would agree with me about you. He was a sensitive man and I live where he did and sleep in his bed and all of you ruined him, drove him to drink and to a perilous act.

How dare you try to take my money away. And you with a wife with ermine, mink, lynx dripping from her plump, sunk shoulders.

Your wife at 312 North Faring Road, Holmby Hills.

Let's be adults, sophisticates. After all, we might not know what we might do if backed against the wall.

—yr lucky penny

It had made more sense when she wrote it than it did now, reading it to them.

Benny patted her shoulder. "So he called the cops on ya, huh?"

"The studio cops. Which is bad enough," Penny said.

They had escorted her from the makeup

department. Everyone had watched, a few of the girls smiling.

"Sorry, Pen," Gordon had said, taking the powder brush from her hand. "What gives in this business is what takes away."

When he'd hired her two months ago, she'd watched as he wrote on her personnel file: M*r*. D.

"Your man, he took this as a threat, you see," Mr. Flant said, shaking his head as he looked at the letter. "He is a hard man. Those men are. They are hard men and you are soft. Like Larry was soft."

Penny knew it was true. She'd never been hard enough, at least not in the right way. The smart way.

It was very late when she left the two men.

She paused before Number Four and found herself unable to move, cold fingertips pressed between her breasts, pushing her back.

That was when she spotted Mrs. Stahl inside the bungalow, fluttering past the picture window in her evening coat.

"Stop!" Penny called out. "I see you!"

And Mrs. Stahl froze. Then, slowly, she turned to face Penny, her face warped through the glass, as if she were under water.

"Dear," a voice came from behind Penny. A

voice just like Mrs. Stahl's. *Could she throw her voice?*

Swiveling around, she saw the landlady standing in the courtyard, a few feet away.

It was as if she were a witch, a shapeshifter from one of the fairytales she'd read as a child.

"Dear," she said again.

"I thought you were inside," Penny said, trying to catch her breath. "But it was just your reflection."

Mrs. Stahl did not say anything for a moment, her hands cupped in front of herself.

Penny saw she was holding a scarlet-covered book in her palms.

"I often sit out here at night," she said, voice loose and tipsy, "reading under the stars. Larry used to do that, you know."

She invited Penny into her bungalow, the smallest one, in back.

"I'd like us to talk," she said.

Penny did not pause. She wanted to see it. Wanted to understand.

Walking inside, she realized at last what the strongest smell in the courtyard was. All around were pots of night-blooming jasmine, climbing and vining up the built-in bookshelves, around the window frame, even trained over the arched doorway into the dining room.

They drank jasmine tea, iced. The room was close and Penny had never seen so many books. None of them looked like they'd ever been opened, their spines cool and immaculate.

"I have more," Mrs. Stahl said, waving toward the mint-walled hallway, some space beyond, the air itself so thick with the breath of the jasmine, Penny couldn't see it. "I love books. Larry taught me how. He knew what ones I'd like."

Penny nodded. "At night, I read the books in the bungalow. I never read so much."

"I wanted to keep them there. It only seemed right. And I didn't believe what the other tenants said, about the paper smelling like gas."

At that, Penny had a grim thought. What if everything smelled like gas and she didn't know it? The strong scent of apricot, of eucalyptus, a perpetual perfume suffusing everything. How would one know?

"Dear, do you enjoy living in Larry's bungalow?"

Penny didn't know what to say, so she only nodded, taking a long sip of the tea. Was it rum? Some kind of liqueur? It was very sweet and tingled on her tongue.

"He was my favorite tenant. Even after..." she paused, her head shaking, "what he did."

"And you found him," Penny said. "That must have been awful."

She held up the red-covered book she'd been reading in the courtyard.

"This was found on....on his person. He must've been planning on giving it to me. He gave me so many things. See how it's red, like a heart?"

"What kind of book is it?" Penny asked, leaning closer.

Mrs. Stahl looked at her, but didn't seem to be listening, clasping the book with one hand while with the other stroked her neck, long and unlined.

"Every book he gave me showed how much he understood me. He gave me many things and never asked for anything. That was when my mother was dying from Bright's, her face puffed up like a carnival balloon. Nasty woman."

"Mrs. Stahl," Penny started, her fingers tingling unbearably, the smell so strong, Mrs. Stahl's plants, her strong perfume—sandalwood?

"He just liked everyone. You'd think it was just you. The care he took. Once, he brought me a brass rouge pot from Paramount studios. He told me it belonged to Paulette Goddard. I still have it."

"Mrs. Stahl," Penny tried again, bolder now, "were you in love with him?"

The woman looked at her, and Penny felt her focus loosen, like in those old detective movies, right before the screen went black.

"He really only wanted the stars," Mrs. Stahl said, running her fingers across her décolletage, the satin of her dressing robe, a dragon painted up the front. "He said their skin felt different. They smelled different. He was strange about smells. Sounds. Light. He was very sensitive."

"But you loved him, didn't you?" Penny's voice more insistent now.

Her eyes narrowed. "Everyone loved him. Everyone. He said yes to everybody. He gave himself to everybody."

"But why did he do it, Mrs. Stahl?"

"He put his head in the oven and died," she said, straightening her back ever so slightly. "He was mad in a way only Southerners and artistic souls are mad. And he was both. You're too young, too simple, to understand."

"Mrs. Stahl, did you do something to Larry?" This is what Penny was trying to say, but the words weren't coming. And Mrs. Stahl kept growing larger and larger, the dragon on her robe, it seemed, somehow, to be speaking to Penny, whispering things to her.

"What's in this tea?"

"What do you mean, dear?"

But the woman's face had gone strange, stretched out. There was a scurrying sound from somewhere, like little paws, animal claws, the sharp feet of sharp-footed men. A gold watch chain swinging and that neighbor hanging from the pear tree.

She woke to the purple creep of dawn. Slumped in the same rattan chair in Mrs. Stahl's living room. Her finger still crooked in the tea cup handle, her arm hanging to one side.

"Mrs. Stahl," she whispered.

But the woman was no longer on the sofa across from her.

Somehow, Penny was on her feet, inching across the room.

The bedroom door was ajar, Mrs. Stahl sprawled on the mattress, the painted dragon on her robe sprawled on top of her.

On the bed beside her was the book she'd been reading in the courtyard. Scarlet red, with a lurid title.

Gaudy Night, it was called

Opening it with great care, Penny saw the inscription:

To Mrs. Stahl, my dirty murderess.
Love, Lawrence.

She took the book, and the tea cup.

She slept for a few hours in her living room, curled on the zebra print sofa.

She had stopped going into the kitchen two days ago, tacking an old bath towel over the doorway so she couldn't even see inside. The gleaming porcelain of the oven.

She was sure she smelled gas radiating from it. Spotted blue light flickering behind the towel.

But still she didn't go inside.

And now she was afraid the smell was coming through the walls.

It was all connected, you see, and Mrs. Stahl was behind all of it. The lightspots, the shadows on the baseboard, the noises in the walls and now the hiss of the gas.

Mr. Flant looked at the inscription, shaking his head.

"My god, is it possible? He wasn't making much sense those final days. Holed up in

Number Four. Maybe he was hiding from her. Because he knew."

"It was found on his body," Penny said, voice trembling. "That's what she told me."

"Then this inscription," he said, reaching out for Penny's wrist, "was meant to be our clue. Like pointing a finger from beyond the grave."

Penny nodded. She knew what she had to do.

"I know how it sounds. But someone needs to do something."

The police detective nodded, drinking from his Coca-Cola, his white shirt bright. He had gray hair at the temples and he said his name was Noble, which seemed impossible.

"Well, Miss, let's see what we can do. That was a long time ago. After you called, I had to get the case file from the crypt. I can't say I even remember it." Licking his index finger, he flicked open the file folder, then beginning turning pages. "A gas job, right? We got a lot of them back then. Those months before the war."

"Yes. In the kitchen. My kitchen now."

Looking through the slim folder, he pursed his lips a moment, then came a grim smile. "Ah, I remember. I remember. The little men."

"The little men?" Penny felt her spine tighten.

"One of our patrolmen had been out there the week before on a noise complaint. Your bookseller was screaming in the courtyard. Claimed there were little men coming out of the walls to kill him."

Penny didn't say anything at all. Something deep inside herself seemed to be screaming and it took all her effort just to sit there and listen.

"DTs. Said he'd been trying to kick the sauce," he said, reading the report. "He was a drunk, miss. Sounds like it was a whole courtyard full of 'em."

"No," Penny said, head shaking back and forth. "That's not it. Larry wasn't like that."

"Well," he said, "I'll tell what Larry was like. In his bedside table we found a half-dozen catcher's mitts." He stopped himself, looked at her. "Pardon. Female contraceptive devices. Each one with the name of a different woman. A few big stars. At least they were big then. I can't remember now."

Penny was still thinking about the wall. The little men. And her mice on their hindfeet. Pixies, dancing fairies.

"There you go," the detective said, closing the folder. "Guy's a dipso, one of his high-class affairs turned sour. Suicide. Pretty clear cut."

"No," Penny said.

"No?" Eyebrows raised. "He was in that oven waist deep, Miss. He even had a hunting knife in his hand for good measure."

"A knife?" Penny said, her fingers pressing her forehead. "Of course. Don't you see? He was trying to protect himself. I told you on the phone, detective. It's imperative that you look into Mrs. Stahl."

"The landlady. Your landlady?"

"She was in love with him. And he rejected her, you see."

"A woman scorned, eh?" he said, leaning back. "Once saw a jilted lady over on Cheremoya take a clothes iron to her fellow's face while he slept."

"Look at this," Penny said, pulling Mrs. Stahl's little red book from her purse.

"*Gaudy Night*," he said, pronouncing the first word in a funny way.

"I think it's a dirty book."

He looked at her, squinting. "My wife owns this book."

Penny didn't say anything.

"Have you even read it?" he asked, wearily.

Opening the front to the inscription, she held it in front of him.

"'Dirty murderess.'" He shrugged. "So you're saying this fella knew she was going to kill him and, instead of going to, say, the police, he writes this little inscription, then lets himself get killed?"

Everything sounded so different when he said it aloud, different than the way everything joined in perfect and horrible symmetry in her head.

"I don't know how it happened. Maybe he was going to go to the police and she beat him to it. And I don't know how she did it," Penny said. "But she's dangerous, don't you get it?"

It was clear he did not.

"I'm telling you, I see her out there at night, doing things," Penny said, her breath coming faster and faster. "She's doing something with the natural gas. If you check the gas jets maybe you can figure it out."

She was aware that she was talking very loudly, and her chest felt damp. Lowering her voice, she leaned toward him.

"I think there might be a clue in my oven," she said.

"Do you?" he said, rubbing his chin. "Any little men in there?"

"It's not like that. It's not. I see them, yes." She couldn't look him in the eye or she would lose her nerve. "But I know they're not really little men. It's something she's doing. It always starts at two. Two a.m. She's doing something. She did it to Larry and she's doing it to me."

He was rubbing his face with his hand, and she knew she had lost him.

"I told you on the phone," she said, more desperately now. "I think she drugged me. I brought the cup."

Penny reached into her purse again, this time removing the tea cup, its bottom still brown-ringed.

Detective Noble lifted it, took a sniff, set it down.

"Drugged you with Old Grandad, eh?

"I know there's booze in it. But, detective, there's more than booze going on here." Again, her voice rose high and sharp, and other detectives seemed to be watching now from their desks.

But Noble seemed unfazed. There even seemed to be the flicker of a smile on his clean-shaven face.

"So why does she want to harm you?" he asked. "Is she in love with you, too?"

Penny looked at him, and counted quietly in her head, the dampness on her chest gathering.

She had been dealing with men like this her whole life. Smug men. Men with fine clothes or shabby ones, all with the same slick ideas, the same impatience, big voice, slap-and-tickle, fast with a back-handed slug. Nice turned to nasty on a dime.

"Detective," she said, taking it slowly, "Mrs. Stahl must suspect that I know. About what she did to Larry. I don't know if she drugged him and staged it. The hunting knife shows there was a struggle. What I do know is there's more than what's in your little file."

He nodded, leaning back in his chair once more. With his right arm, he reached for another folder in the metal tray on his desk.

"Miss, can we talk for a minute about *your* file?"

"My file?"

"When you called, I checked your name. S.O.P. Do you want to tell me about the letters you've been sending to a certain address in Holmby Hills?"

"What? I . . . There was only one."

"And two years ago, the fellow over at MCA? Said you slashed his tires?"

"I was never charged."

Penny would never speak about that, or what that man had tried to do to her in a back booth at Chasen's.

He set the file down. "Miss, what exactly are you here for? You got a gripe with Mrs. Stahl? Hey, I don't like my landlord either. What, don't wanna pay the rent?"

A wave of exhaustion shuddered through Penny. For a moment, she did not know if she could stand.

But there was Larry to think about. And how much she belonged in Number Four. Because she did, and it had marked the beginning of things. A new day for Penny.

"No," Penny said, rising. "That's not it. You'll see. You'll see. I'll show you."

"Miss," he said, calling after her. "Please don't show me anything. Just behave yourself, okay? Like a good girl."

Back at Number Four, Penny laid down on the rattan sofa, trying to breathe, to think.

Pulling Mrs. Stahl's book from her dress pocket, she began reading.

But it wasn't like she thought.

It wasn't dirty, not like the brown-papered ones. It was a detective novel, and it took place in England. A woman recently exonerated for poisoning her lover attends her school reunion. While there, she finds an anonymous poisoned pen note tucked in the sleeve of her gown: "You Dirty Murderess . . . !"

Penny gasped. But then wondered: Had that inscription just been a wink, Larry to Mrs. Stahl?

He gave her books she liked, Benny had said. *Stiff British stuff that he could tease her about.*

Was that all this was, all the inscription had meant?

No, she assured herself, sliding the book back into her pocket. It's a red herring. To confuse me, to keep me from finding the truth. Larry needs me to find out the truth.

It was shortly after that she heard the click of her mail slot. Looking over, she saw a piece of paper slip through the slit and land on the entry-way floor.

Walking over, she picked it up.

Bungalow Four:
You are past due.
—Mrs. H. Stahl

"I have to move anyway," she told Benny, showing him the note.

"No, kid, why?" he whispered. Mr. Flant was sleeping in the bedroom, the gentle whistle of his snore.

"I can't prove she's doing it," Penny said. "But it smells like a gas chamber in there."

"Listen, don't let her spook you," Benny

said. "I bet the pilot light is out. Want me to take a look? I can come by later."

"Can you come now?"

Looking into the darkened bedroom, Benny smiled, patted her forearm. "I don't mind."

Stripped to his undershirt, Benny ducked under the bath towel Penny had hung over the kitchen door.

"I thought you were inviting me over to keep your bed warm," he said as he kneeled down on the linoleum.

The familiar noise started, the *tick-tick-tick*.

"Do you hear it?" Penny said, voice tight. Except the sound was different in the kitchen than the bedroom. It was closer. Not inside the walls but everywhere.

"It's the igniter," Benny said. "Trying to light the gas."

Peering behind the towel, Penny watched him.

"But you smell it, right?" she said.

"Of course I smell it," he said, his voice strangely high. "God, it's awful."

He put his head to the baseboards, the sink, the shuddering refrigerator.

"What's this?" he said, tugging the oven forward, his arms straining.

He was touching the wall behind the oven, but Penny couldn't see.

"What's what?" she asked. "Did you find something?"

"I don't know," he said, his head turned from her. "I . . . Christ, you can't think with it. I feel like I'm back in Argonne."

He had to lean backward, palms resting on the floor.

"What is it you saw, back there?" Penny asked, pointing behind the oven.

But he kept shaking his head, breathing into the front of his undershirt, pulled up.

After a minute, both of them breathing hard, he reached up and turned the knob on the front of the oven door.

"I smell it," Penny said, stepping back. "Don't you?"

"That pilot light," he said, covering his face, breathing raspily. "It's gotta be out."

His knees sliding on the linoleum, he inched back toward the oven, white and glowing.

"Are you . . . are you going to open it?"

He looked at her, his face pale and his mouth stretched like a piece of rubber.

"I'm going to," he said. "We need to light it."

But he didn't stir. There was a feeling of

something, that door open like a black maw, and neither of them could move.

Penny turned, hearing a knock at the door.

When she turned back around, she gasped.

Benny's head and shoulders were inside the oven, his voice making the most terrible sound, like a cat, its neck caught in a trap.

"Get out," Penny said, no matter how silly it sounded. "Get out!"

Pitching forward, she leaned down and grabbed for him, tugging at his trousers, yanking him back.

Stumbling, they both rose to their feet, Penny nearly huddling against the kitchen wall, its cherry-sprigged paper.

Turning, he took her arms hard, pressing himself against her, pressing Penny against the wall.

She could smell him, and his skin was clammy and gooosequilled.

His mouth pressed against her neck roughly and she could feel his teeth, his hands on her hips. Something had changed, and she'd missed it.

"But this is what you want, isn't it, honey?" the whisper came, his mouth over her ear. "It's all you've ever wanted."

"No, no, no," she said, and found herself

crying. "And you don't like girls. You don't like girls."

"I like everybody," he said, his palm on her chest, hand heel hard.

And she lifted her head and looked at him, and he was Larry.

She knew he was Larry.

Larry.

Until he became Benny again, moustache and grin, but fear in that grin still.

"I'm sorry, Penny," he said, stepping back. "I'm flattered, but I don't go that way."

"What?" She said, looking down, seeing her fingers clamped on his trouser waist. "Oh. Oh."

Back at Number Three, they both drank from tall tumblers, breathing hungrily.

"You shouldn't go back in there," Benny said. "We need to call the gas company in the morning."

Mr. Flant said she could stay on their sofa that night, if they could make room under all the old newspapers.

"You shouldn't have looked in there," he said to Benny, shaking his head. "The oven. It's like whistling in a cemetery."

A towel wrapped around his shoulders, Benny was shivering. He was so white.

"I didn't see anything," he kept saying. "I didn't see a goddamned thing."

She was dreaming.

"You took my book!"

In the dream, she'd risen from Mr. Flant's sofa, slicked with sweat, and opened the door. Although nearly midnight, the courtyard was mysteriously bright, all the plants gaudy and pungent.

Wait. Had someone said something?

"Larry gave it to me!"

Penny's body was moving so slowly, like she was caught in molasses.

The door to Number Four was open, and Mrs. Stahl was emerging from it, something red in her hand.

"You took it while I slept, didn't you? Sneak thief! Thieving whore!"

When Mrs. Stahl began charging at her, her robe billowing like great scarlet wings, Penny thought she was still dreaming.

"Stop," Penny said, but the woman was so close.

It had to be a dream, and in dreams you can do anything, so Penny raised her arms high, clamping down on those scarlet wings as they came toward her.

The book slid from her pocket, and both of

them grappled for it, but Penny was faster, grabbing it and pushing back, pressing the volume against the old woman's neck until she stumbled, heels tangling.

It had to be a dream because Mrs. Stahl was so weak, weaker than any murderess could possibly be, her body like that of a yarn doll, limp and flailing.

There was a flurry of elbows, clawing hands, the fat golden beetle ring on Mrs. Stahl's gnarled hand against Penny's face.

Then, with one hard jerk, the old woman fell to the ground with such ease, her head clacking against the courtyard tiles.

The ratatattat of blood from her mouth, her ear.

"Penny!" A voice came from behind her.

It was Mr. Flant standing in his doorway, hand to his mouth.

"Penny, what did you *do*?"

Her expression when she'd faced Mr. Flant must have been meaningful because he had immediately retreated inside his bungalow, the door locking with a click.

But it was time, anyway. Of that she felt sure.

Walking into Number Four, she almost felt herself smiling.

One by one, she removed all the tacks from her makeshift kitchen door, letting the towel drop onto her forearm.

The kitchen was dark, and smelled as it never had. No apricots, no jasmine, and no gas. Instead, the tinny smell of must, wallpaper paste, rusty water.

Moving slowly, purposefully, she walked directly to the oven, the moonlight striking it. White and monstrous, a glowing smear.

Its door shut.

Cold to the touch.

Kneeling down, she crawled behind it, to the spot Benny had been struck by.

What's this? he'd said.

As in a dream, which this had to be, she knew what to do, her palm sliding along the cherry-sprig wallpaper down by the baseboard.

She saw the spot, the wallpaper gaping at its seam, seeming to breathe. Inhale, exhale.

Penny's hand went there, pulling back, the paper glue dried to fine dust under her hand.

She was remembering Mrs. Stahl. *I put up fresh wallpaper over every square inch after it happened. I covered everything with wallpaper.*

What did she think she would see, breathing hard, her knees creaking and her forehead pushed against the wall?

The paper did not come off cleanly, came off in pieces, strands, like her hair after the dose Mr. D. passed to her, making her sick for weeks.

A patch of wall exposed, she saw the series of gashes, one after the next, as if someone had jabbed a knife into the plaster. A hunting knife. Though there seemed a pattern, a hieroglyphics.

Squinting, the kitchen so dark, she couldn't see.

Reaching up to the oven, she grabbed for a kitchen match.

Leaning close, the match lit, she could see a faint scrawl etched deep.

The little men come out of the walls. I cut off their heads every night. My mind is gone.
Tonight, I end my life.
I hope you find this.
Goodbye.

Penny leaned forward, pressed her palm on the words.

This is what mattered most, nothing else.

"Oh, Larry," she said, her voice catching with grateful tears. "I see them, too."

The sound that followed was the loudest

she'd ever heard, the fire sweeping up her face.

The detective stood in the center of the courtyard, next to a banana tree with its top shorn off, a smoldering slab of wood, the front door to the blackened bungalow, on the ground in front of him.

The firemen were dragging their equipment past him. The gurney with the dead girl long gone.

"Pilot light. Damn near took the roof off," one of the patrolman said. "The kitchen looks like the Blitz. But only one scorched, inside. The girl. Or what's left of her. Could've been much worse."

"That's always true," the detective said, a pillow of smoke making them both cover their faces.

Another officer approached him.

"Detective Noble, we talked to the pair next door," he said. "They said they warned the girl not to go back inside. But she'd been drinking all day, saying crazy things."

"How's the landlady?"

"Hospital."

Nobble nodded. "We're done."

It was close to two. But he didn't want to go

home yet. It was a long drive to Eagle Rock anyway.

And the smell, and what he'd seen in that kitchen—he didn't want to go home yet.

At the top of the road, he saw the bar, its bright lights beckoning.

The Carnival Tavern, the one with the roof shaped like a big top.

Life is a carnival, he said to himself, which is what the detective might say, wryly, in the books his wife loved to read.

He couldn't believe it was still there. He remembered it from before the war. When he used to date that usherette at the Hollywood Bowl.

A quick jerk to the wheel and he was pulling into its small lot, those crazy clown lanterns he remembered from all those years ago.

Inside, everything was warm and inviting, even if the waitress had a sour look.

"Last call," she said, leaving him his rye. "We close in ten minutes."

"I just need to make a quick call," he said.

He stepped into one of the telephone booths in the back, pulling the accordion door shut behind him.

"Yes, I have that one," his wife replied, stifling a yawn. "But it's not a dirty book."

Then she laughed a little in a way that made him bristle.

"So what kind of book is it?" he asked.

"Books mean different things to different people," she said. She was always saying stuff like that, just to show him how smart she was.

"You know what I mean," he said.

She was silent for several seconds. He thought he could hear someone crying, maybe one of the kids.

"It's a mystery," she said, finally. "Not your kind. No one even dies."

"Okay," he said. He wasn't sure what he'd wanted to hear. "I'll be home soon."

"It's a love story, too," she said, almost a whisper, strangely sad. "Not your kind."

After he hung up, he ordered a beer, the night's last tug from the bartender's tap.

Sitting by the picture window, he looked down into the canyon, and up to the Hollywood sign. Everything about the moment felt familiar. He'd worked this precinct for twenty years, minus three to Uncle Sam, so even the surprises were the same.

He thought about the girl, about her at the station. Her nervous legs, that worn dress of hers, the plea in her voice.

Someone should think of her for a minute, shouldn't they?

He looked at his watch. Two a.m. But she won't see her little men tonight.

A busboy with a pencil moustache came over with a long stick. One by one, he turned all the dingy lanterns that hung in the window. The painted clowns faced the canyon now. Closing time.

"Don't miss me too much," he told the sour waitress as he left.

In the parking lot, looking down into the canyon, he noticed he could see the Canyon Arms, the smoke still settling on the bungalow's shell, black as a mussel. Her bedroom window, glass blown out, curtains shuddering in the night breeze.

He was just about to get in his car when he saw them. The little men.

They were dancing across the hood of his car, the canyon beneath him.

Turning, he looked up at the bar, the lanterns in the window, spinning, sending their dancing clowns across the canyon, across the Canyon Arms, everywhere.

He took a breath.

"That happens every night?" he asked the busboy as the young man hustled down the stairs into the parking lot.

Pausing, the busboy followed his gaze, then nodded.

"Every night," he said. "Like a dream."